JAMES IN A MESS
and Other Thomas the Tank Engine Stories

Based on *The Railway Series* by the Rev. W. Awdry

Photographs by David Mitton, Kenny McArthur, and Terry Perm.
for Britt Allcroft's production of *Thomas the Tank Engine and Friends*

A Random House PICTUREBACK®

Library of Congress Cataloging-in-Publication Data
James in a mess and other Thomas the tank engine stories / photographs by David Mitton, Kenny McArthur, and Terry Permane for Britt Allcroft's production of Thomas the tank engine and friends.   p.   cm. — (A Random House pictureback) "Based on The Railway series by the Rev. W. Awdry." Summary: Sir Topham Hatt's railroad engines, Harold the helicopter, and Bertie the bus learn about good manners and hard work. ISBN 0-679-83895-3 (trade pbk.) [1. Railroads—Trains—Fiction. 2. Behavior—Fiction.]   I. Mitton, David, ill.   II. McArthur, Kenny, ill. III. Permane, Terry, ill.   IV. Awdry, W. Railway series.   V. Thomas the tank engine and friends.
PZ7.J1557 1993 [E]—dc20 92-25654
Manufactured in the United States of America   10 9 8 7

RANDOM HOUSE 🏠 NEW YORK

James in a Mess

Toby and Henrietta were enjoying their new job on the Island of Sodor, but they do look old-fashioned and did need new paint.

James was very rude whenever he saw them. "Yecch! What dirty objects!" he would say.

At last Toby lost patience. "James," he asked, "why are you red?"

"I am a splendid engine," answered James, "ready for anything. You never see my paint dirty."

"Oh!" said Toby innocently, "that's why you once needed bootlaces—to be ready, I suppose."

James went redder than ever and snorted off. It was such an

insult to be reminded of the time a bootlace had been used to mend a hole in his coaches.

At the end of the line, James left his coaches and got ready for his next train. It was a "slow freight," stopping at every station to pick up and set down cars.

James hated slow freight trains. "Dirty cars from dirty sidings! Yecch!"

Starting with only a few, he picked up more and more cars at each station till he had a long train.

At first, the freight cars behaved well, but James bumped

them so crossly that they were determined to get back at him.

Presently, they approached the top of Gordon's hill. Heavy freight trains halt here to set their brakes. James had had an accident with cars before and should have remembered this.

"Wait, James, wait," said the driver, but James wouldn't wait. He was too busy thinking what he would say to Toby when they next met.

The freight cars' chance had come.

"Hurrah! Hurrah!" they laughed, and banging their buffers, they pushed him down the hill.

"On! On!" yelled the cars.

"I've got to stop, I've got to stop," groaned James.

Disaster lay ahead.

Something sticky splashed all over James. He had run into two tar wagons and was black, from smoke box to cab. He was more dirty than hurt, but the tar wagons and some cars were all to pieces.

Toby and Percy were sent to help and came as quickly as they could.

"Look here, Percy!" exclaimed Toby. "Whatever is that dirty object?"

"That's James. Didn't you know?"

"It's James's shape," said Toby, "but James is a splendid red engine, and you never see his paint dirty."

James pretended he hadn't heard.

Toby and Percy cleared away the unhurt cars and helped James home.

Sir Topham Hatt met them.

"Well done, Percy and Toby." He turned to James. "Fancy letting your cars run away. I *am* surprised. You're not fit to be seen; you must be cleaned at once. Toby shall have a new coat of paint."

"Please, sir, can Henrietta have one too?" said Toby.

"Certainly, Toby."

"Oh, thank you, sir! She will be pleased."

All James could do was watch Toby as he ran off happily with the news. ●

Bertie's Chase

"Stop, stop! I've got Thomas's passengers!" wailed Bertie, roaring up to the gates. It was no good. Edward was gone.

"Bother," said Bertie. "Bother Thomas's fireman not coming to work today. Why did I promise to help the passengers catch the train?"

"That will do, Bertie," said his driver. "A promise is a promise, and we must keep it."

"I'll catch Edward or bust," said Bertie.

"Oh, my gears and axles," he groaned, toiling up the hill. "I'll never be the same bus again.

"Hurray! Hurray! I see him," cheered Bertie as he reached the top.

"Oh, no! Edward's at the station. No...he's stopped at a crossing—Hurray! Hurray!"

Bertie tore down the hill.

"Well done, Bertie!" shouted his passengers. "Go it!"

Bertie skidded into the yard. "Wait! Wait!" cried Bertie. He was just in time to see Edward puff away. "I'm sorry," said Bertie.

"Never mind," said the passengers. "After him, quickly—third time lucky, you know. Do you think we'll catch him at the next station, Driver?"

"There's a good chance," replied the driver. "Our road keeps close to the line, and we can climb hills better than Edward. I'll just make sure." He spoke to the stationmaster. Bertie and the passengers waited impatiently.

"Yes, we'll do it this time," said the driver.

"Hurray," called the passengers as Bertie chased after Edward once more.

"This hill is too steep! This hill is too steep!" grumbled the coaches as Edward snorted in front.

They reached the top at last and ran smoothly into the station.

"Peee-eep!" whistled Edward. "Get in quickly, please."

The conductor blew the whistle, and Edward's driver looked back. But the flag didn't wave. Then he heard Bertie.

Everything seemed to happen at once—and the stationmaster told the conductor and driver what had happened.

"I'm sorry about the chase, Bertie," said Edward.

"My fault," replied Bertie. "Late at Junction…you didn't know…about Thomas's passengers."

"Peep peep! Good-bye, Bertie, we're off," whistled Edward.

"Three cheers for Bertie!" called the passengers.

Bertie raced back to tell Thomas that all was well.

"Thank you, Bertie, for keeping your promise," said Thomas. "You're a very good friend indeed." ●

Percy and the Signal

Percy works in the yard at the big station. He loves playing jokes, but they can get him into trouble.

One morning he was very cheeky indeed. "Peep peep! Hurry up, Gordon! The train's ready."

Gordon thought he was late.

"Ha ha ha!" laughed Percy, and showed him a train of dirty coal trucks.

Gordon thought how to get back at Percy for teasing him.

Next it was James's turn.

"Stay in the shed today, James. Sir Topham Hatt will come and see you."

"Ah!" thought James. "Sir Topham Hatt knows I'm a fine engine. He wants me to pull a Special Train."

James's driver and fireman could not make him move. The other engines grumbled dreadfully. They had to do James's work as well as their own.

At last the inspector arrived. "Show a wheel, James. You can't stay here all day."

"Sir Topham Hatt told me to stay here. He sent a message this morning."

"He did not. How could he? He's away for a week."

"Oh!" said James. "Oh! Where's Percy?" Percy had wisely disappeared!

When Sir Topham Hatt came back, he was cross with James and Percy for causing so much trouble.

But the very next day Percy was still being cheeky. "I say, you engines, I'm to take some freight cars to Thomas's junction. Sir Topham Hatt chose me especially. He must know I'm a Really Useful Engine."

"More likely he wants you out of the way," grunted James.

Gordon looked across to James. They were going to play a trick on Percy.

"James and I were just speaking about signals at the Junction. We can't be too careful about signals. But then I needn't say that to a Really Useful Engine like you, Percy."

Percy felt flattered.

"We had spoken of 'backing signals,'" put in James. "They

need extra special care, you know. Would you like me to explain?"

"No thank you, James," said Percy. "I know all about signals."

Percy was a little worried. "I wonder what 'backing signals' are?" he thought. "Never mind, I'll manage." He puffed crossly to his freight cars and felt better.

He came to a signal. "Bother! It's at 'danger.'"

The signal moved to show 'line clear.' Its arm moved up instead of down. Percy had never seen that sort of signal before.

"Down means 'go' and up means 'stop,' so upper still must mean 'go back.' I know! It's one of those 'backing signals' that Gordon told me about."

"Come on, Percy," said his driver, "off we go. Stop! You're going the wrong way."

"But it's a backing signal," Percy protested and told him about Gordon and James. The driver laughed and explained.

"Oh dear!" said Percy. "Let's start quickly before they see us."

He was too late. Gordon saw everything.

That night the big engines talked about signals. They thought the subject was funny! Percy thought they were being very silly! ◉

Percy Proves a Point

Percy worked hard at the new harbor. The workmen needed stone for their building. Toby helped, but sometimes the loads of stone were too heavy, and Percy had to fetch them for himself. Sometimes he'd see Thomas.

"Well done, Percy. Sir Topham Hatt is very pleased with us."

An airfield was close by. Percy heard the airplanes zooming overhead all day. The noisiest of all was a helicopter.

"Silly thing!" said Percy. "Why can't it go and buzz somewhere else?"

One day Percy stopped at the airfield. "Hello!" said Percy. "Who are you?"

"I'm Harold. Who are you?"

"I'm Percy. What whirly great arms you've got."

"They're nice arms," said Harold. "I can hover like a bird. Don't you wish *you* could hover?"

"Certainly not—I like my rails, thank you."

"I think railways are slow," said Harold. "They're not much use and quite out of date." He whirled his arms and buzzed away.

Percy found Toby at the quarry. "I say, Toby—that Harold, that stuck-up whirlybird thing, says I'm slow and out of date. Just let him wait, I'll show him."

He collected his freight cars and started off, still fuming.

Soon they heard a familiar buzzing.

"Percy," whispered his driver, "there's Harold. He's not far ahead. Let's race him."

"Yes, let's!" said Percy.

Percy pounded along. The cars screamed and swayed.

"Well, I'll be a ding-dong-danged!" said the driver. There was Harold — the race was on!

"Go it, Percy!" he yelled. "You're gaining."

Percy had never been allowed to run fast before. He was having the time of his life.

"Hurry! Hurry! Hurry!" he panted to the cars.

"We don't want to; we don't want to," they grumbled. It was no use. Percy was bucketing along with flying wheels, and Harold was high and alongside.

The fireman shoveled for dear life.

"Well done, Percy," shouted the driver. "We're gaining! We're going ahead! Oh, good boy, good boy!"

A "distant signal" warned them that the harbor wharf was near. *Peep, peep, peep!*

"Brakes, Conductor, please." The driver carefully checked the train's headlong speed.

They rolled under the main line and halted on the wharf.

"Oh dear!" groaned Percy. "I'm sure we've lost."

The fireman scrambled to the cab roof. "We've won! We've won!" he shouted. "Harold's still hovering. He's looking for a place to land!"

"Listen, boys!" the fireman called. "Here's a song for Percy:

Said Harold the Helicopter to our Percy, 'You are slow!
Your Railway is out of date and not much use, you know.'
But Percy with his stone cars did the trip in record time,
And we beat the helicopter on our old Branch Line."

Percy loved it. "Oh, thank you!" he said. He liked the last line
best of all and was a very happy engine. ◉